The Caged Birds
of Phnom Penh

BY FREDERICK LIPP

ILLUSTRATED BY
RONALD HIMLER

HOLIDAY HOUSE · NEW YORK

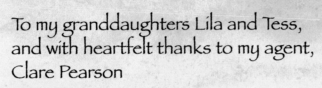

To my granddaughters Lila and Tess,
and with heartfelt thanks to my agent,
Clare Pearson

—F. L.

To Kate and John

—R. H.

Text copyright © 2001 by Frederick Lipp
Illustrations copyright © 2001 by Ronald Himler, Inc.
All Rights Reserved
Printed in the United States of America
www.holidayhouse.com
The text typeface is Nofret Light.
The medium of the artwork is watercolor and gouache over pencil.
First Edition

Library of Congress Cataloging-in-Publication Data
Lipp, Frederick
The caged birds of Phnom Penh / by Frederick Lipp; illustrated by Ronald Himler.—1ˢᵗ ed.
p.   cm.
Summary: A young Cambodian girl saves her money to buy a bird
on which to make a wish for her poor family's future.
ISBN 0-8234-1534-1
[1. Cambodia—Fiction. 2. Wishes—Fiction.] I. Himler, Ronald, ill. II. Title.
PZ7.L6646 Cag 2001
[E]—dc21   99-052625

A yellow wind blew softly through the rice fields outside the city of Phnom Penh.
Winds were yellow in Cambodia when they joined sunshine and sudden rains.
They brought lush growth, and bowls of rice for children.

Ary had lived all of her eight years along the busy city streets. Every day, she ate salt-fish and rice. But she never saw where the rice grew. The merchants told her stories about the green world outside the capital city. They said there were birds outside the city that flew free, birds as colorful as a thousand kites soaring against the blue sky.

By the time the yellow winds reached Phnom Penh, they had mixed with smoke from charcoal fires and exhaust from motorcycles. The yellow winds grew gray. Gray winds were difficult to breathe.

One burning day, Ary awakened early. She dug her hands under the sleeping mat and grasped the three hundred riels she had earned selling strings of flowers to tourists. As her mother and father slept on the floor near her three brothers and her two older sisters, she slipped quietly out the open door. She ran to the old part of the city, called Wat Phnom Penh. Here, by the Buddhist temple, merchants were setting up shop while the tourists ate breakfast in their plush hotels and guest houses.

The bird lady greeted Ary with a sly smile.

"Little girl, why are you along the great steps at this hour? You have nothing to sell the tourists?"

"Not today," said Ary. "This morning I have come to buy a little bird from your cage. I want to set it free, so my wishes for my family may come true."

"That is the custom," the bird lady replied. "But little girl, dreams are for the rich and powerful. You have no money, so run along home."

The bird lady tilted her cage forward. A hundred birds fed on little seeds and drank from a small dish. They perched on bamboo rods stuck through the wire cage. In this crowded world far from the fresh yellow winds, the birds sang. Ary eyed the little prisoners. There was a shrill, high-pitched sadness in their song, like the feeling she often felt.

"I have saved three hundred riels," said Ary.

She placed the money into the old woman's hand. The bird lady fingered the coins as she rocked back and forth on her haunches.

"Choose your bird, little girl, and make a wish."

Ary reached her hand through the small, wire mesh door. The birds danced on the bamboo perches, crowding together as she searched further in their little prison.

Ary softly closed her fingers around one little bird that backed into a corner. The frightened creature, with opened beak, gasped for air. Ary felt its rapid heartbeat.

"Hurry. Make your wish and let the bird go," said the bird lady. "The birds can die of fright if you don't release them quickly."

Wishes rose in Ary's mind, the way goldfish swim to the pond's surface in search of food. She raised her hand. The bird pecked at her finger for release. As she offered it to the sky, Ary made her wishes.

At first the bird soared straight past rooftops and trees. Ary sighed, relieved that it was free. The bird circled overhead. With wings outstretched, it soared on the hot air currents rising from the streets.

"Fly, little one. Stretch your wings and carry my wishes so they may come true," Ary whispered.

She was so happy, she was laughing. The three hundred riels was a small price to pay for this great moment.

The bird lady said nothing. She rocked back and forth on her haunches, waiting.

Then it happened, as it had happened a thousand times before. The bird turned in the direction of the bird lady and slowly descended from the sky, the way a leaf falls from a tree.

Ary cried, "No! Keep flying! Remember the yellow wind."

The bird settled on the bird lady's finger. She opened the cage, and the little bird hopped onto a bamboo perch. It took up the song of the jailed birds. High pitched. Strained. Lonely, although the bird was surrounded by others.

The old woman rocked back and forth, waiting for the next customer.

Ary knew her wishes would not come true. She knew any bird that could not fly free would never be a bearer of good fortune. The bird had grown accustomed to the prison. Food and water were plentiful in the wire cage.

Ary cried.

She cried while running as fast as she could back home. She slipped through the open door while her family was still sleeping. This is our cage, Ary thought as she lay her head on the mat. I was tricked by the bird lady. Nothing changes here. Salt-fish and rice. Tattered clothes. Doors open to flies. I wish we could grow wings and fly far from this place. Lift our wings and fly anywhere....

"*Anywhere*," Ary said out loud.

Ary was surprised by her anger, and her outburst stirred her family from their sleep. Her youngest brother, Serey, whose name means 'born free,' rubbed his eyes and then squinted.

"Ary, what's wrong?" he whispered.

Ary was too troubled to speak.

Serey reached over from his sleeping mat to touch his sister gently on the shoulder.

They both looked through the open door into the blinding morning light. Another day began for their family in the streets of Phnom Penh.

Even though the days that followed were much like any others, Ary never gave up her hope to make her family's world better.

One day, after selling strings of blossoms along the Mekong river, Ary asked her grandfather, "Tell me, how many wishes is one person allowed at a time?"

The old man thought to himself.

"You may have as many wishes as you are able to make on a single breath of air. Take a deep breath. Then blow outward like the wind. Let all the wishes ride on a single breath."

Ary thought she had many more wishes for her family than could ride on a single breath.

"One more thing you must remember, Ary. Answers to wishes rarely come in the manner we expect."

"Tell me, Grandfather, do you believe letting a caged bird go free makes wishes come true?"

"Yes, my lovely child, but only if you find the blessed bird."

"The blessed bird. How does one find the right bird in a cage of one hundred?"

Her grandfather smiled. "Ary, remember your name means 'knowledge'." He said not another word.

At the end of each day, Ary saved a few coins for herself and gave the rest
to her father. Ary, in spare hours, watched the caged birds.

At first they all looked the same, but after days of watching, she noticed that
every bird had a personality. Some were shy. Others were bullies. She remembered
her grandfather's words. Not one looked like the blessed bird, the one to make her
wishes come true.

Early one morning, Ary watched the bird lady put a new bird into the cage.
It immediately fluttered into the corner, too afraid to eat or drink. The bird held
a secret long forgotten by the other birds.

The next day before dawn, Ary slipped from her sleeping mat and ran
to the temple steps. The bird lady was there with her cage of one hundred birds.
She rocked back and forth, waiting for the first customers.

"I have come for another bird," said Ary.

"Go away. And don't think I haven't seen you watching me these past days,"
said the bird lady.

"But I have money, four hundred riels for that little bird in the corner," Ary said.

"Any bird in the cage but that one," said the bird lady.

By this time Ary was used to the bird lady's tricks. Ary threw up her hands,
clutching the money tightly. She shook her head and then, disgusted, said, "Keep
your birds. I know another seller along the Mekong river."

She turned. It was an old street trick used to buy rice and it usually worked,
though it was risky.

She walked three steps away when she heard the old woman say, "Go ahead,
choose any bird in the cage. Remember, the one in the corner is sick. It will die
if you choose it. Sick."

Ary paid the money. She slipped her hand through the little door. The new bird, still trembling, did not struggle to get out of her way. She lifted the bird in the palm of her hand until she was able to stroke it lightly with the tip of her finger.

She felt the bird's heart beat like a drum. Ary kissed the bird on the head. She raised it slowly to the sky, drawing at the same time her deepest breath. As she slowly opened her fingers, the bird hesitated for a moment and then, with wings beating downward, flew from Ary's hand.

Ary slowly released her single breath, adding wishes to the bird's flight.
"I wish for my family curry chicken, new clothes, work for my brother...."
She was running out of breath.
"I wish the police would not bother us. I wish to find an ointment
for Grandfather's sores...."
And on the last gasp of air, realizing she had not wished one thing
for herself, Ary spoke two last words: "More knowledge." She had
always dreamed of going to school, and then one day to the university.

The little bird flew in a great circle around the square.

The bird lady sneered. Ary laughed and jumped up and down, shouting, "Fly, little one! Fly where the wind is yellow and the land is green. Fly with wishes on your wings. Fly!"

The little bird grew smaller and smaller in the sky as it moved into the east, where the sun was a yellow sliver, a lemon rind of dawn. Ary knew in her heart somehow, in some way, her wishes would come true. The form they would take was as uncertain as the new day.